W9-CDN-288

BOUNDLESS SKY

Amanda Addison

Manuela Adreani

Fountaindale Public Library District
300 W. Briarcliff Rd.
Bolingbrook, IL 60440

LANTANA
PUBLISHING

Nobody knew,
nobody dreamed,
nobody even considered the possibility
that a bird which fits in your hand
might fly halfway round the world—
and back again.

One September morning,
Alfie went into the garden.
The air was cool. Autumn was coming.
"Good morning, Bird!" said Alfie.
She fluttered her wings and with a nod
to Alfie, off she flew.

Bird flew low,
over the golden fields.
She swooped and soared and raced the
kite runners along the sand.
"Goodbye! See you in the spring!"
called a girl from the shore.
Bird flapped her wings to say farewell.

Over the blue sea,
circling the ferries, ships and fishing boats.
Everyone turned their heads,
"Off they go, flying south for the wintertime!"
said a mother to her son.

The flock roosted in the safety of the reed beds
before flying higher, higher,
up and over the snow-capped mountains
to a village.
The children said hello,
and soon they waved goodbye.

Across the desert,
the hardest part of the journey.
Hungry and thirsty, Bird flew on
and at last reached an oasis.
A girl called Leila said, "Bird! Welcome to my home! Drink!"
"Thank you, child," said Bird.

Flying high through the jungle canopy
in a cloud of butterflies,
to the river
where the waters raced, explosions of spray,
and through it Bird came
shooting across the river and onwards.

Over the grasslands and plains
and the lake was finally in view.
Bird was home.

Soon enough, summer in Africa was ending.
Bird flew over the lake;
the children waved goodbye.
Over grasslands,
over plains.
Back over the jungle,
back across the mighty desert.

Bird reached the oasis.
Bird looked for Leila.
"Where are you?" she called.
No sign of Leila.
A thirsty Bird flew on.

She skirted the big ocean,
drunk up the spray
when...
An almighty storm blew up from nowhere.

Exhausted, Bird landed in the mountain village
where she rested.
Then...

Back over fields.
Back across the sea.
Back across the beach.
Over the fields,
to the town.

One April morning,
Leila stood in her new garden.
The air was warm. Spring was on its way.
"Good morning, Bird!" said Leila.
"Leila! You are many miles from home."

Across the fence, stood Alfie.
"Hello Bird. Hello Leila. Welcome everyone!"

For Warwick Bradshaw, with love, and for Norwich, City of Sanctuary.
Amanda

For everyone I've met on my journeys and for those I'm yet to meet!
Manuela

First published in the United Kingdom in 2020 by Lantana Publishing Ltd., London.
www.lantanapublishing.com

American edition published in 2020 by Lantana Publishing Ltd., UK.
info@lantanapublishing.com

Text © Amanda Addison, 2020
Illustration © Manuela Adreani, 2020

The moral rights of the author and illustrator have been asserted.

All rights reserved. No part of this publication may be reproduced, stored in a retrieval system,
or transmitted in any form or by any means, electronic, mechanical, photocopying, recording or
otherwise, without the prior written permission of the copyright owner.
A CIP catalogue record for this book is available from the British Library.

Distributed in the United States and Canada by Lerner Publishing Group, Inc.
241 First Avenue North, Minneapolis, MN 55401 U.S.A.
For reading levels and more information, look for this title at www.lernerbooks.com
Cataloging-in-Publication Data Available.

Printed and bound in China.
Original artwork using pencils, finished digitally.

ISBN: 978-1-911373-67-4
eBook ISBN: 978-1-911373-70-4